Little Red Riding Hood

For all the big bad wolves

Copyright © 1995 by Mireille Levert
First paperback edition 1996

Groundwood Books/Douglas & McIntyre Ltd.
585 Bloor Street West, Toronto, Ontario M6G 1K5

Distributed in the U.S. by **Publishers Group West**
4065 Hollis Street, Emeryville, CA 94608

The publisher gratefully acknowledges the assistance of the Canada Council and the Ontario Arts Council.

Canadian Cataloguing in Publication Data

Main entry under title:
Little Red Riding Hood

"A Meadow Mouse paperback".
ISBN 0-88899-272-6

1. Fairy tales – Germany. I. Levert, Mireille.

PZ8.L68 1996   j398.2'094302   C96-930312-2

The illustrations are done in watercolours
Printed and bound in Hong Kong by Everbest Printing Co., Ltd.

Little
Red
Riding
Hood

BY

Mireille Levert

A Meadow Mouse Paperback

Groundwood Books / Douglas & McIntyre

TORONTO / VANCOUVER / BUFFALO

nce upon a time there was a dear little girl who was loved by everyone who knew her. Her grandmother loved her most of all, and she could never do enough for the child. She gave her a cape made of red velvet, and it looked so sweet that the little girl never wanted to wear anything else. So everyone began to call her Little Red Riding Hood.

One day Little Red Riding Hood's mother said, "Take this cake and bottle of wine over to your grandmother. She is sick and weak and this will be good for her. Go straight there and don't leave the path. Otherwise you'll fall, and the bottle will break."

"I'll do everything just as you say," Little Red Riding Hood promised.

Grandmother lived deep in the forest, a half hour's walk from the village. As soon as Little Red Riding Hood entered the woods, she met a wolf. She had no idea what a vicious beast he was, and she wasn't afraid.

"How are you, Little Red Riding Hood?" he said.

"I'm fine, thank you, Wolf."

"And where are you going so early?"

"To visit my sick grandmother."

"What are you carrying in that basket?"

"I'm taking cake and wine to help her get well."

"But, Little Red Riding Hood, where does your grandmother live?"

"About fifteen minutes from here, under three large oak trees. You must know the place."

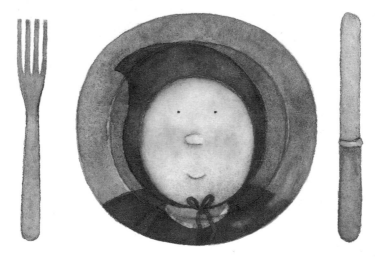

What a young, tender thing, the wolf thought to himself. She'll make a plump little morsel—better-tasting than the old lady. If I am clever about this, I'll be able to eat them both.

The wolf walked beside Little Red Riding Hood, and after awhile he said, "Little Red Riding Hood, you're marching along as if you're on your way to school. You aren't even noticing how lovely it is here in the woods. Listen to how beautifully the birds are singing! Look at the pretty flowers!"

Little Red Riding Hood looked around, and when she saw the sunbeams dancing through the trees and the beautiful flowers everywhere, she thought, I will pick a fresh bouquet for Grandmother. It's still early. I have plenty of time.

So she left the path to gather flowers. But each time she picked one, she saw a prettier flower just a little farther off, and she walked deeper and deeper into the forest.

Meanwhile, the wolf went straight to Grandmother's house and knocked on the door.

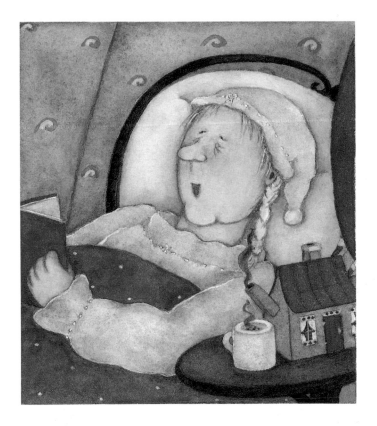

"Who's there?"

"It's Little Red Riding Hood with cake and wine.
Please open the door."

"Just lift the latch and come in," called Grandmother.
"I'm too weak to get up."

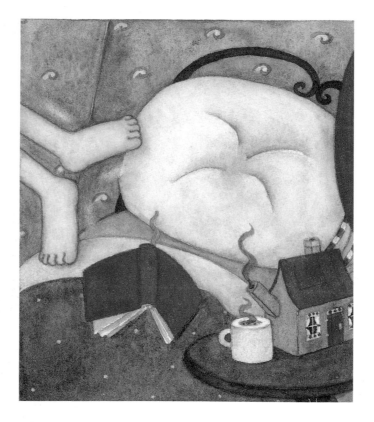

The wolf lifted the latch and the door swung open. Without a word he went straight to Grandmother's bed and swallowed her. Then he put on her nightdress and nightcap and climbed into bed.

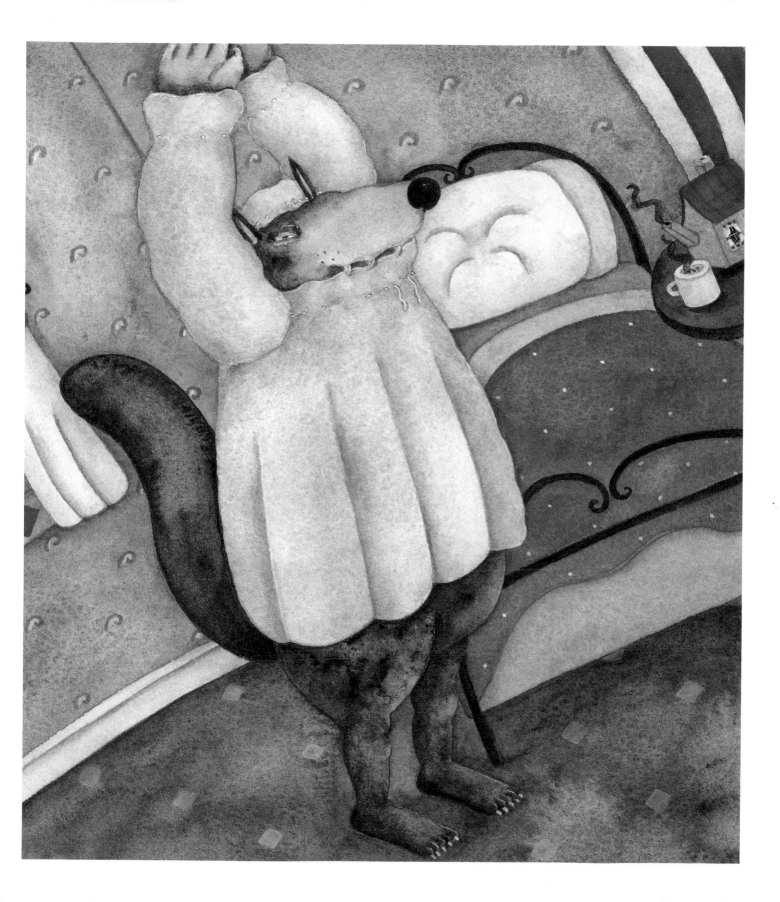

Not far away, Little Red Riding Hood was still busy
picking flowers. When she had more than she could carry,
she remembered her grandmother and set out on her way
again.

As she approached the house, she was surprised to see
that the door was open. Why do I feel so frightened, she
thought as she walked inside. I should be happy to be here
at Grandmother's.

"Good morning, Grandmother," she called, but there
was no answer. Then she went over to the bed. There lay
Grandmother, her nightcap pulled down over her face. She
was looking quite peculiar.

"Grandmother," Little Red Riding Hood said, "what big ears you have."

"The better to hear you with."

"And, Grandmother, what big eyes you have."

"The better to see you with."

"But, Grandmother, what big hands you have."

"The better to hold you with."

"Oh, Grandmother, what an awfully big mouth you have."

"The better to eat you with!"

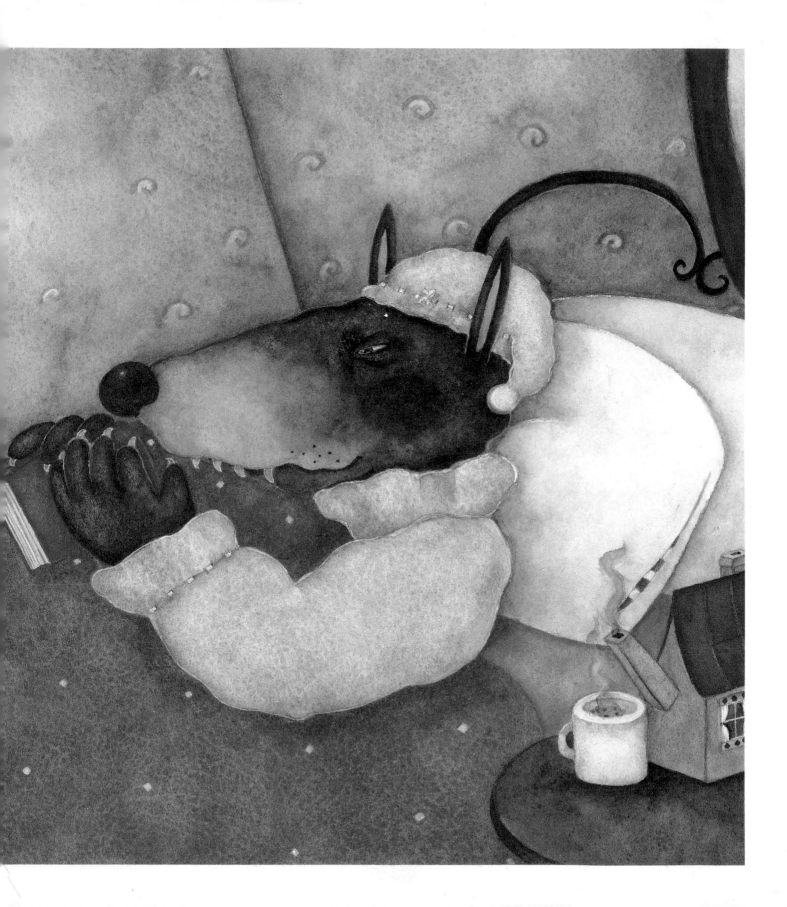

And no sooner had the wolf said that
than he leapt out of bed and gobbled up
poor Little Red Riding Hood!

Then he lay down in bed again, fell asleep and began to snore.

Outside, a hunter was passing by. "Listen to the old lady snore," he said. "I'd better see if anything's wrong."

He walked into the house, and when he came to the bed he saw the wolf, fast asleep.

"Here you are, you old sinner," he said, aiming his rifle. "I've been looking for you for a long time."

He was just about to shoot when it occurred to him that the wolf could have eaten the grandmother and that she might be saved. So he put down his rifle, took a pair of scissors and began to cut open the wolf's stomach.

After a few cuts he saw a bright red hood, and soon out jumped Little Red Riding Hood.

"Oh, it was so dark in there!" she cried.

Then out came the old grandmother, and she was alive, too.

Little Red Riding Hood went outside. She gathered up some big stones and filled the wolf's stomach with them. When he woke up, he tried to run away, but the stones were so heavy that he fell down and died.

The hunter skinned the wolf and took home the fur. Grandmother ate the cake and drank the wine that Little Red Riding Hood had brought, and soon she was well again.

As for Little Red Riding Hood, she said to herself, "Never again will I leave the path and go into the forest when my mother has told me not to."